DISNEP

My First Stories

MERRY CHRISTMAS, CHIP AND DALE

W9-BFM-903

An imprint of Phoenix International Publications, Inc.

Chicago • London • New York • Hamburg • Mexico City • Sydney

On the night before Christmas, Mickey and his friends are busy getting ready for the holiday.

A curious Chip and Dale watch through the window. Minnie waves hello and invites them inside.

"Let's go in and help," says Chip.
"And maybe have a little fun," Dale says with a giggle.

"Can you help me decorate Daisy's Christmas cookies?" Donald asks.

"Yum!" says Chip.
"We love cookies," says Dale.

"Those cookies are for Santa," says Daisy. "Say, two are missing! Donald, did you eat two cookies?"

Chip and Dale giggle to each other with their mouths full.

"Do you want to help me decorate?" asks Goofy.

"You bet!" says Chip.

Chip and Dale grab some garland and wrap it around Goofy.

"Just a second, fellas," says Goofy. "We need to decorate the tree, not me!"

"It's time for the finishing touch!" calls Mickey. "Let's put the star on top."
"Oh, boy!" says Dale.
"Here we come!" says Chip.

"We finished decorating," says Mickey. "Let's play outside!"

"But where are Chip and Dale?" asks Minnie.

"And why are the stockings giggling?" asks Goofy.

"Christmas decorating is fun!" says Chip.

"We don't have any decorations for our home," says Dale.

"We'll fix that in a jiffy!" says Goofy. "Let's start with some twinkle lights."

Minnie and Daisy collect pine cones
and ribbon to make garlands.

"Awww," says Chip, as he throws
a snowball at Dale. "So pretty!"

Mickey offers his old mittens to use as stockings.

"This mitten would make a great sled," says Chip.

"Wheeee!" says Dale.

"We need one last thing," says Chip.

"A Christmas tree for you and me!" says Dale.

The friends take a tiny tree branch and turn it into a little Christmas tree with holly leaves, red berries, and acorn ornaments!

Mickey invites everyone back to his house for hot chocolate.

"We had a lot of fun today," says Chip.

"What should we do tomorrow?"
asks Dale.
"Celebrate Christmas!" says Mickey.
"Merry Christmas, Chip and Dale!"